Anna Roth

I Have a Dream

Scent of Roses
of Life

Anna Roth

I Have a Dream

Scent of Roses
of Life

Impressum:

© 2015 by Anna Roth

Proofreading, composition and coverdesign:
Angelika Fleckenstein; spotsrock.de
Translation: Uschi Mirwald
Illustrations: Bettina Roth
Coverpicture: © by Larissa Dening; 123rf Fotos
Pictures inside the book by photographers at pixabay.com

Verlag: tredition GmbH, Hamburg

ISBN   978-3-7323-1587-1 (Paperback)
           978-3-7323-1588-8 (Hardcover)
           978-3-7323-1589-5 (e-Book)

Printed in Germany

For my Beloved Family

Introduction

The scent of roses of life
accompanies me through the day
and embraces me during the night.
It saturates the everyday life
and gives requiescence to the soul.
It deludes any worries
with its fragrance,
so that they
almost vanish
into thin air.

It provides ideas
to create life,
to fathom the ego,
to reinvent the self.

Thus I wish you,
while inhaling this
scent of roses
many new inspirations
that make life
worth living.

***

Anna Roth
Königswinter, August 30th, 2013

Table of contents

Introduction 9

Ars amandi (The Art of Love) 17

Breath of Love 20

Bridge of Life 21

Carpe Diem (Seize the Day) 23

Childhood Dreams 24

Dice of Life 26

Dreams of a Tie 27

Dress of Roses 29

End - Decision 31

Faith - Hope - Love 33

Farewell Benedetto 34

Francis 36

Freedom 37

Genius 38

God Save the Queen 40

I Love You 42

I Meets You 45

Knowing without Knowing 46

Mozarttorte (Mozart Cake) 48

Multitask 49

My Guardian Angel 50

Nolens Volens 51

Oh, Grant me a Smile 52

Panta rhei - Everything Flows 53

Pas-de-Deux (A Step for Two) 55

Present Time 56

Prince George Alexander Louis of Cambridge... 57

Recognize - Think - Want - Do.................................. 58

Resurrection... 59

Rose of Life... 60

Scent of Roses of Life.. 61

Sissi.. 63

Sky Meets Sea... 65

Sleep of the Soul.. 66

Soul of Scent of Roses.. 67

Spell of Love... 68

Tea of Roses of Life... 69

Tête-à-tête... 70

The Die is Cast... 72

They Did not Know - That they Do not Know 73

Think Positively.. 77

Truth.. 78

Vastness... 80

Vienna.. 81

Vis-á-Vis.. 82

Waltz of Roses... 84

Whisper of Roses.. 85

Willem Alexander & Maxima................................ 87

Wisdom.. 88

Word of Roses... 90

About the Author.. 92

Ars amandi (The Art of Love)

Is it an art - being able to love?
Or is it a gift - being able to love?
Can only the one give love
who has been loved before?
Does being loved
precede the ability to love?

Let us look into the eyes
of a happy child,
allowed to experience a lot of love
and still does.

Already now this little child
gratifies us
by smiling at us.
Its happiness - is our happiness.

We put all our love
into the little child,
to form
a loving being.
Thus enriched
the little child grows up
and later then,
as an adult
he feels an inner desire
to share
the gift of love

devote himself - giving himself away
and immersed in this happiness
he thinks back to his childhood.

And all the love
he experienced,
all the love
he was given,
he wants to share.

And thus is growing from anew
a little child
that, beloved and blessed
may behold the world.
This way Ars amandi bestows
all generations
and likes to stay
where love is lived,
where the heart is given freely
and thus widens the view

towards God
who embodies love,
who guides the world,
nourishes it with His love
and instils it in the human heart

and therewith breaks the evil
so that Ars amandi
may rule the world.

***

Breath of Love

Your breath of love
permeates my being,
gives me wings,
deeply immerses
into my soul

so that it bounces
and sings deeply inside of me,
brings sound
to the breath of love
that arises from Your love
for me.

✦✦✦

Bridge of Life

Is there a bridge of life
everyone has to cross,
that carries us through everyday life,
even in spite of disappointment and distress?

Is it different for each of us?
Must we practice walking on it,
or will it shift us into a square
from which we try to escape throughout our lives?
Or will we learn to love our bridge?

Or will we build our own bridge
and give it our shape,
in accordance to our standard of life,
so that it wears our face,
so that it carries our weight
with grief and sorrow
and daily hassles
but also with hope
for our tomorrow?

If it is too high
we shall not succeed.
If it is too narrow
we will fall.

*Thus is it wise
to give our bridge of life the dimension
that truly equals our life,
so that we can properly walk on it,
as it bends to our volition
so that we may create our ought.*

***

Carpe Diem (Seize the Day)

Carpe diem - seize the day -
is easily said.
What exactly does it mean?

Should I only tackle
without thinking,
only steer my activities
to the "Now"?

Or may I also rest at times,
doing nothing at all,
though the spirit inside of me is active,
makes me cogitate
and plan calmly,
shows me priorities
which, implemented into the ought
should carry out
the "Carpe diem".

So that Carpe diem
will not agitate us,
but give precedence
to logic.

***

Childhood Dreams

Do you remember
the dreams of your childhood,
floating through the air,
passing clouds,
high up to the stars,
to greet the moon,
to meet the sun?

During the day you were creating
your own world,
in the sandbox
beneath the firmament.

You saw the birds
flying high above,
or swaying
in the treetops.

Then in the evening,
next to your little bed
sat mummy
who lovingly took you
into her arms

and delighted you
with a fairy tale,
prayed with you
and sent you your angel
to watch
over you
and to always protect
your paths.

Then, in gentle peace
your eyes
gradually shut.

And with a smile you dozed off
into a dream
of being a princess
in beautiful robes,
with a golden crown,
where prince charming comes
to lead you to the throne.

Where you live
happily together
in your heavenly castle
forever.

✳✳✳

Dice of Life

Does it exist,
the dice of life
where not in vain
you throw the dice
for your daily fortune?

Or do you throw in vain,
captivated by the moment?

Or has your life
already been diced,
before you were able to act on your own?

No - this should not happen!
As a free being
you yourself dice your life.

You are free to give
the dice
a new impetus,
arise - to a new number!

Try it-
and take heart,
have trust,
why -
should it not turn out - all right?

***

Dreams of a Tie

Mirror, mirror on the wall,
who is the fairest one in the land of ties?

Each morning from anew
hope awakes:
Am I going to take part today?

Will I please him,
or are my stripes too wide
so that again he is not willing
to wear me,
although he once
wanted to possess me?

For so long I have been hanging in the closet.
My girlfriend is also quite sick,
as she never sees the light of day
but has to stay in the closet.

Thus we sadly look at each other,
if there is nothing we can do about it?
Yes - we forge out a plan.

We are going to completely reinvent ourselves.
Will splotch each other
in a screaming bright squaring.

And - look,
early next morning
it catches his gaze.

Then, on the spur of the moment
the tie man puts on
one of the two,
so that the other one thinks:
For sure - it will be my turn tomorrow.

***

Dress of Roses

Do we all wear a dress of roses,
not knowing - not assuming
how it affects the inside
and appears to the outside?

Are we encompassed by the rose
that enchants us -
carries us away
from the daily grey?

Or do we even walk
in dresses of roses
which do not suit us,
which we want to change?

Or are we surrounded
by a secret
that accompanies us
our whole life

whose solution
we do not find,
since we cannot
fathom ourselves
down to the
depths of the soul?

*The rose remains
wrapped in silk,
does not reveal
its identity.*

*It tenderly flutters in the wind
and leaves open the question of -
who we are.*

*But one thing is for sure -
a beloved child
of God.*

✳ ✳ ✳

End - Decision

There is still time.
The clock still ticks.
For how long?
Seconds only?

You can still change
your fate.
You can still plead:
Take me
up to where You are -
forgive me.

Not always
have I been good to You.
Not always
did I believe in You.
I often had doubts:
are You real?

Often the question arose:
what is going to happen to me?
Is there a later,
once I leave this place?

Is there a life
after death?
Should I dare
to confess my guilt,

rely on You
loving me,
hoping that
despite of everything
You will grant me one last chance?

Oh You, my dear God,
what happens inside of me?
The longing
I never experienced
now draws me -
lovestruck
towards You.

Though too weak
to breathe a word,
my heart speaks out to You:
Forgive me.

***

Faith - Hope - Love

These three divine virtues
accompany us throughout our life,
once we let them
into our heart.

And if we believe
that God exists.
And if we hope
that He will always forgive us.
And if we trust in Him
and build on His love
that He will never withdraw.

Then He will accompany us
into death,
and with Him through it
to lead us
towards Him.

For alone with Him
we find the happiness
which is perfect,
which gives meaning
to our being.

***

Farewell Benedetto

Farewell Benedetto -
parting hurts,

the step came too unexpectedly
and anyway,
who can still understand?

For - are you not
the rock in turbulent waters?

Your theology counts.
We can count on it,
firmly trust in it.

Your teaching is teaching-
not emptiness.

You are our teacher,
our father
and our advisor

You have the perspective
and universally rule with foresight
your church folk.

Who else could do -
as you can?

God gave you the grace,
the ability
and now -
you walk away,
leave us behind.
You have surely conferred
your step with God.

Your place becomes vacant.
Who will take over?
Will he faithfully
keep his promise
solely
to conform
the will of God,
also against and
despite of resistance?

Thus we now want
to bethink ourselves
and render our requests
to God.

***

Francis

Hello Francis,
are you the Pope
everybody has to go with?

Who elucidates the hearts
with one word,
who opens the view,
away from the inessential
towards that
what really counts.

We have been well-nourished for too long
have walked the path of convenience,
burdened with ballast
God was not pleased with.

Thus you now guide us
up the steep path,
to rebuild
our church.

***

Freedom

We need freedom
for our dreams,
for our longing
that fills our heart
and appeases our hunger,

hunger for security,
hunger for a little bit of time,
for the things
we love,
for the things
that are individually
solely
written in our hearts.

And please,
let it happen
that little bit of dreaming,
and give yourselves
a little bit of time,

to dive into
and to taste
the freedom
which awaits us
in eternity.

***

Genius

You are a genius.
Perhaps you do not know it
or do not want to know it;
nevertheless it is obvious
that you, as a genius
are also always eccentric.

Only like this you can put
a face to your work,
onlythis way it can bear
your face,
your identity.

Your soul leaves and enters
your creation.
Your self becomes empty,
to fill your creation.

This way your self transcends -
into the It.
You constantly live
in a border process,
in an emotional misery
between life and death.

Will you be able
to catch up with yourself
and regenerate into your self
and yet
leave upon your creation -
your face?

***

God Save the Queen

Elizabeth the second
that is what you are called,
and you are known to the world
as dutiful.

Already at young age
you had to act,
to rule
thereupon as the Queen.

By your side
Prince Philip, your husband.
He keeps you grounded
in difficult times

hence you do not carry alone
the load of the crown,
no - together
the two of you look after
the good of your people.

Yet you were never
spared from any sorrow,
whether within the family - whether from the state.
You know no rest,
move forward courageously,
being a role model to your people.

Despite difficult times
you keep your strength for humour.
Thus you celebrate
with your people
who thank you in return
with cheerful hymns.

Thus we keep wishing you
"God Save the Queen"

✲✲✲

I Love You

*I love you
speaks the soul.*

*You are my everything
You my self.*

*Without you - it does not work.
Without you - my heart breaks.
Without you - I am not myself.
Without you - I lose myself.*

***

I Meets You

Without you - No me.
You infuse my face.
Without you - I cannot find myself.

You alone - are the track
upon which I lose myself
to get closer to me
inside of you.

Because a self
that only refers to itself
dissolves
into nothing,

cannot stay
the way it is,
will then
fall apart
to end
as nothing,

also leaves
no track,
is reduced to
remain as "Only".

***

Knowing without Knowing

As we were flying
past the years,
we were like dreamers
everything – was irrespective to us.

We wanted to make everything better
and knew everything better,
and did not realize
that we did not know,
that we are ignorant.

Meanwhile, our way unfortunately lead us
past the solution,
because we gave
only our knowledge
into the dough of formula for life.

Until, after lots of vagaries
then finally prepared
to know about our ignorance,
and to mix from anew the dough of formula for life
with external knowledge,

to open it, complement it,
to spice it, shape it,
until it rose
and inside of it
the diverse facets of life
could fully unfold.

***

Mozarttorte (Mozart Cake)

If you are in Vienna,
this beautiful city
with its diverse
historic splendour,

then please taste it
before leaving,
the delicious Mozart cake,
local here
at this place.

You will never forget it,
as quietly, imperceptibly fine
it sends
traces of desire
into your heart.

This is how it should be,
how it should stay,
for Mozart cake and Vienna
belong together,
cannot let go
of each other.

***

Multitask

Help - I am able to multitask;
an iPad on the left - the iPhone on the right side,
eyes turned towards the TV,
simultaneously and specifically in my view
the new style program by click,

immediately on the double followed by
trying a latte,
eating a baguette,
simultaneously inhaling the news.

Then, after four minutes,
targeting a new project which,
albeit distant, I can quickly reach
via motorway.

Oh - I see the sky blue.
The sun is shining - I realize it.
Life is beautiful - this is how I like it.

Enjoying to the fullest
moments of happiness for seconds
which are, still pulsing after hours
deep inside my soul

and give me as a multitask
the secure feeling -
my life has a meaning.

***

My Guardian Angel

Since childhood
I can ask my angel
and tell him my worries.

He was sent to me from God,
to accompany me through my life,
to protect and guide me,

save me from danger,
to then quietly tell me
where God wants me to be.

Follow me - I will then carry you
courageously through all dangers,
so that both of us
will safely reach Him together some day.

***

Nolens Volens

(Willy-Nilly)

Isn't our whole life
all willy-nilly?
We do not want to, yet want to?
We want to, yet do not want to?

We do not know what is right.
Finally a doubt is left behind:
will we find our happiness in life?

Or does such a happiness in life not exist,
so that it does not matter
whether we choose nolens or volens?

In the end, only one thing will count:
what we made out of our talent.

Did we make use of it -
did we take care of it?
Have we also made mistakes?

For without them, maturity will not become real.
The Yes to our No – a must-be.

We confess our weaknesses,
as only out of it may grow
the seed of being itself -
our real self.

***

Oh, Grant me a Smile

Oh, grant me a smile
only for an instant
and, behold, heaven unfolds,
leads us back to happiness.

Endows peace to our souls,
bestows confidence to the being,
casts off the grey of worries,
invites us to hope.

Here we forge plans
and regain courage,
to walk new paths
believing - it will be well.

***

Panta rhei - Everything Flows

Are we embedded in the flow of life
and hence always in motion towards something?

Our life flows, even while we are asleep.
What - if we do not want this
and just stand still
and run on the spot
and do not want to go further?

Will the flow of life seize us
so that we must swim in it?

If that is how it is - would it have a meaning
and would move our being
and give it a direction.

Nevertheless, would we then be free
to also swim against it?
Or would we be out of our senses,
wanting to determine ourselves
to escape the flow of life -
give it a different direction
that better adapts to our life?

*Thus the flow of life continues to flow
and remains our companion,
even if we determine the direction ourselves,
we will never be able
to entirely escape it.*

***

Pas-de-Deux (A Step for Two)

Is the step as a pair easier
as the step on your own?
Is it more difficult to be lonely?

Does the pas-de-deux
bring the drive into our life?
Does it give us the rhythm
so that we can take easier
what is fact?

Does it make us happy?
Do we fly
in a pas-de-deux
through our
ought of life as such?

Then yes please -
the two of us
take each other by the hand
and soar up
in a pas-de-deux
into the Promised Land.

There we look back once again
with a smile.
Yes, indeed -
the pas-de-deux
bestows happiness in life.

***

Present Time

What do we understand by "Present Time"?
Do we feel exposed to it?
Do we have to act in the present?
Can't some things be allowed to happen later?

Surely this is not how it is meant.
Because present time,
as each time, is a time
that seems already over.
For present -
is only an instant
that quickly carries off
always leading us to the next,

once arrived here -
it is already over.
Thus we are standing in a three-fold:
In the present - past - and still ahead.

Therefore it is wise - to do our thing
and not to rush by the clock,
so that we will not only in a run
fully respect the present time,

But go quiet and pause,
be inspired and guided
by the wisdom of the spirit
that shows us the scheme of life

which then does not adjust to time,
but places itself above it,
embedding it
into the life of the world.

***

Prince George Alexander Louis of Cambridge

Long-awaited - finally here
Prince George - the superstar.
On the 22nd of July 2013
he came into this world.

A whole nation celebrates
with Kate & William
in the warm glow of the sun.

They made it -
heavenly perfect,
the royal baby smiles
and warms the hearts.

May the joy never end
and the happiness never change,
and God send His blessings,

hold them in His hands,
so that William & Kate, without sorrow
can walk with little George towards tomorrow.

✫✫✫

Recognize - Think - Want - Do

We can only think
what we realized,
and only want
what we thought.

All action is considered to be
the fruit of trinity,
even though much is done automatically,
as firmly anchored in everyday life,
dealt with routinely.

Nevertheless new knowledge
takes its time
until it is understood -
and can be considered.

The will
then puts it into practice,
if it does not want
the idea to repose.

***

Resurrection

In every life
there is resurrection,
resurrection
after the descent
into nothing.

You feel
like you cannot go on,
as if the world is
against you?

But then
all of a sudden
a light
shines forth!

You grant
your being
a new view,
the tunnel opens.

Sanguinely
you walk
into the day -
leaving behind you
the night.

***

Rose of Life

What does the rose of life stand for?
Are we always in its view?
Does it accompany us through life
or does it discretely withhold?

What is its distinctive mark?
Does it announce itself through its fragrance?
Or does it want to give us freedom
and not direct our steps
as long as we think wisely?

But once we stray
off the path,
it then tenderly
breathes upon us
for to
captivate us,

so that,
with a safe feeling
we will
achieve the goal of life.

Scent of Roses of Life

The scent of roses of life
how does it smell,
how does it taste,
do we notice it at all?

Or does it approach
and then permeate us
with its perfume,
that only the you within my self
can perceive?

In contrast, the me within my self
does not notice it,
for the fragrance of life
has to disengage
from the narrowness of the self,
to reinvent itself
and to widen the narrowness,
looking for the you.

Here it wants to incarnate,
to include, and thus
intensify and
capture us
in its scent,

breathe on us and export,
so that the self
only wants one thing:
get lost inside the you
within the scent of roses of life.

***

Sissi

Your life did not advance
in straight succession
The pain of living
hit you early,

leaving inside of you
the longing
which, till the end
pierced your heart.

Broken - disappointed
you completely lost yourself,
despite of all the splendour of life
you also knew,
you also loved.

But, in the end
there was nothing left for you.
Even hope
gradually disappeared.

Disappointedly you gave in,
on the surface -
but your inside -
the world did not know.

May the Lord
transform your pain
and generously
quench your longing,

which the world
cannot assuage,
which will only substantiate
once you reach HIM.

✳✳✳

Sky Meets Sea

There, where the sky touches the sea,
there, where the wave washes around the sand,
there, where the seagull breaks the silence,
there, where the rock glows in the light,

there, where the soul gets lost in God,
and its love for Him is born anew,
there, where the eye experiences the vastness
and nourishes itself from the
paradisiacal beauty,

there, let us stay
and never more haste,
there, let us build our cottage
and entrust ourselves to Him
to take a glimpse from time
into eternity.

***

Sleep of the Soul

Is there a sleep of the soul
that brings peace?
Or does it put an end to you,
as only the soul
revives you,

lifts your heart
to the joyful sound,
like the birds
the heavenly singing?

Is the soul able to sleep?
Has it not been given immortality
which moves the human life,
sets free within it a higher quest
away from itself - towards Him?

This way the soul can never be at rest.
It constantly seeks
to do good in a human,
to illuminate his way,
so that in the end
he will not miss his target.

***

Soul of Scent of Roses

How is it to be imagined,
the soul of the scent of roses?
Does it exist?
This cannot be -
or can it?

For the soul, after all,
is the being itself.
And doesn't its perfume prove
that it exists?

Incessantly it sheds
its love
to the grey of earth,
and bestows to it
a touch of idyll

in the play of colours
of sky-blue,
in the fragrant garment
of the abundance of spring.

And thus it permeates
the dough of earth
that, very gently,
frees the human

from the constraint of earth
and lifts him up
to heaven.

***

Spell of Love

Spell of Love
dream of yearning
touch me
and
unlock me,

pervade me
and stay with me,
do not abandon me,
do not leave me.

Be a part
of my self,
until one day
my eyes will glaze over.

✻✻✻

Tea of Roses of Life

Do you know the tea of roses of life
that gives your daily life a little leisure,
that waits to be tasted,
just to be savoured?

Indulge in it
and stay with it;
then it will inspire you
from anew
and will motivate you

to step out
beyond your limits
that you have imposed on yourself.

It will encourage you,
give you strength
to attempt a new beginning,
even after many years.

✳✳✳

Tête-à-tête

(Rendezvous)

Between Faith and Reason

Can the belief
in God be rational?
Or do we only
credulously imagine

that a God
must exist,
who loves us,
who forgives us,
who draws us up towards Him,
though we do not deserve it?

What does reason think?
Does it only think superficially
that - what is real,
that - what exists,
that - what it can fathom?

Or is it free
to think beyond itself
towards Him?

And does not allow limitation
to that, what is visible,
to that, what the world thinks,
to that, what science
unscientifically draws the view to?

Then it is on the right path.
Then God bestows it with His grace
to realize
that the world does not stand on its own
that it surpasses
beyond reason,

that divine wisdom
does not preclude
the human mind,
but reveals

a new path
in the light of faith
and reason,

a path -
that n e v e r ends,
that dilates us, frees us
from the narrowness of our thinking,

that immerses us
in His wisdom
which we can n e v e r seamlessly
think through,
but may only taste a bit.

A more delicious dish
does not exist!

***

The Die is Cast

The die is cast.
The number fallen.

Yesterday is sealed.
Today dawns

and enters the tomorrow
and quietly also rolls the dice

and lays the trail for the path
that will only start tomorrow.

✳ ✳ ✳

They Did not Know - That they Do not Know

They did not know
that they do not know
and do not wish for
more knowledge,
as they thought
they knew it all

and did not realize
their knowledge
to meanwhile be -
ignorance.

Thus they did not find
the solution
and remained
on the spot
and could not
go any further,
and could no longer escape
their ignorance.

As they did not question
their knowledge,
and kept the door locked
against new knowledge,

they did not perceive
their ignorance,
and did not want to know
what they do not know.

✭✭✭

Think Positively

Think positively,
direct your thoughts
towards hope,
not looking for the rub
that disturbs hope.

No - consistently
pursue your goal,
consistently
take small steps
and you shall rise
from your lethargy.

Even if there sometimes is
a reverse:
Look ahead
and keep in view
what is happening.

Then you experience the vastness,
step out of the narrowness,
become happy, are content,
please - proceed.

***

Truth

What is truth?
What everybody individually
recognizes as true -
is that truth?

Is truth that - what exists?
But doesn't that what exists
look differently to everybody?

Thus truth
cannot be viewed individually,
as otherwise
it would leave us standing in the rain.

We would not be able to move forward
with it
for, firmly anchored
inside of us, the law
precisely helps us perceive true and false
and to distinguish between them.

We clearly know
about the truth inside of us
and should face up to it.

*It appears both friendly
and welcoming,
and wants to lead us
towards its realm of truth.*

*Thus we are
free in our choice
and may constantly decide
from anew.*

✳✳✳

Vastness

You are lying on the beach,
listening to the sound of the waves.
You see the vastness of the sea
and never ever want
to let it go,
never ever set a limit
to your life,

Add vastness to your daily life;
reshape your future life.
Hoist it from the frame,
step out of the narrowness,
Give it a new impetus,

realize your dreams
and no longer lose time
for demarcation of life,
create a new start for yourself.

Generously draw the view
to what pleases you
and opens toward you
and hence -

gives you new strength
away from you -
towards the you -
the meaning of life.

***

Vienna

Vienna - city of my dreams.
I am longing for you,
even if I am rarely here,
you are my love
you and your magnificent cafés,

the St. Stephen's Cathedral,
the Opera House and the history,
Mozart greets from afar
with his sublime melody.

Even Goethe looks at me wisely,
I very well
remember Werther.

The whole flair of the city
captivates my heart.
Thus I will gladly be back
as soon as I can.

***

Vis-á-Vis

Reason meets faith

Can faith and reason
walk together
or is one of those two
left standing in the rain?

Do they have to be opposites
or may they
rejoice in a common origin?

Does reason have anything
in common with truth
if its being
will delight in the good,

consider prudence,
direct justice,
explore courage,
find the right measure
in life.

Didn't He give us the spirit
for being able to think?
Why should then
reason direct us
away from the faith
we were given by Him.

Don't both need to re-invent themselves
to fathom their minds towards Him?

✯✯✯

Waltz of Roses

Its blossoms flutter to the music
and that is a fact.

Tenderly they swirl around us,
the rose petals – silently,
and gently catch us
into their essence,

so that we spin around with them,
simply leave work undone.
For this spell of the waltz of roses
we cannot resist.

***

Whisper of Roses

Two roses meet.
They recognize each other by scent.
The same harmony
refines the air.

The same soil
brought them both forth.
Joy arises.
Tenderly they breathe
a secret
into each other's ear.

Till the end of their days
they want to stay
closely together;
and not let go
the one - the other.

Yes, they want to
give themselves away and please each other
and never part.
Because this red blossom
and this scent
constantly ignites
their love for each other.

They want to die together
with a smile,
once their time
has come,
so that their grace
even in death
will not fade.

✳✳✳

Willem Alexander & Maxima

What a couple!
They take the hearts by storm.
The Royal Crown is restored to its full splendor.

The monarchy is well-grounded,
for both are loved by the people.
And nothing can surpass this love - ever!

And thus joyfully
a whole nation celebrates:
Long may it shine,
the royal throne.

Everybody rejoices
from near and far,
long live -
our beloved royal couple
Willem Alexander & Maxima

***

Wisdom

Wisdom only sets up its tent
in silence.
It has its home
inside the heart.

Guided by the soft voice
it is easily ignored,
since often drowned
by the noise of the world.

Also what it offers
sounds modest,
as it is not at all
a child of the time.

More other worldly -
so we think,
is where it is trying to guide us.
We are to act
beyond space and time.

But this is a fallacy,
for, after all, it is precisely it
that exactly knows the world
and - isn't it its superstructure?

Does it not hold it in its hand
to define the end at the final stage;
in order to then reshape it -anew and beautifully
according to its plan?

Therefore it is smart and wise
to listen to its soft voice,
for wisdom
is a great gift.

It cannot be learned
and consequently not be acquired
like science.

No -
it should be humbly implored
and begged for,
for only the Holy Spirit
alone
admits it to enter ourselves.

So it quietly knocks
at the door of our heart:
Will we let it in?

***

Word of Roses

Softly it reverberates inside of you -
accompanies you -here and there,
does not wander from place to place,
no - it is yours.

It is only meant for you.
Even while you are dreaming - it watches over you.

Only your heart understands the sound,
only inside of you - it reaches you.

You have the spiration - solely you,
You have the key - let it in,
so that it can work inside of you
and enchant you -
throughout your life.

***

About the Author

Anna Roth, born in Cologne.
The author, living in the vicinity of Bonn, is a graduated theologian, married and mother of five children; in addition, she has seven grandchildren. She studied RC theology in Bonn, Vallendar and Sankt Augustin. The focus of her writing activity are Mariology and poetry. Furthermore she writes Mariological publications for various journals. She lectures at channel K-TV television and often hosts readings and lectures in her own house, under the name of: **"Literatursofa"**. There she will also start a new series of seminars "Positive Lebensgestaltung" (positive ideas for shaping one's life) as of autumn 2014.

Series on channel K-TV:
MARIA Immaculata conceptio: 3 parts
MARIA Assumpta: 3 parts
FATIMA topical: 6 parts
FATIMA and the mercy of God: 4 parts

Appearances on Television
Channel K-TV: 2008 - 2010, 2013
German Literature Channel: 2010-2014

Readings / Book Launches

Book Fair Frankfurt   2011
Book Fair Frankfurt   2012
Book Fair Frankfurt   2013
Book Fair Leipzig   2012
Book Fair Vienna   2012
Book Fair Karlsruhe   2013

Readings and lectures in the house of Mrs. Roth

2012:

Readings: **Scent of roses of love, Part 1**
Readings: **Scent of roses of love, Part 2**

2013:

Lectures:
Literatursofa:

Die End-Entscheidung
(The final decision)

Tod trifft Leben – Was geschieht mit uns nach dem Tod?
(Death meets life - What will happen to us after death?)

Religionen im Vergleich:
Christentum – Hinduismus – Buddhismus
(Religions by comparison: Christianity – Hinduism – Buddhism)

Maria - auch Deine Mutter
(Mary - your mother as well)

2014:

Readings and lectures:
Literatursofa:

Großes Lyrik-Potpourri
(Great poetry-potpourri)

Die vier Kardinaltugenden
(The four cardinal virtues)

Religionen im Vergleich:
Christentum – Judentum – Islam
(Religions by comparison:
Christianity – Judaism – Islam)

Lebensgestaltung mit Maria
(Shaping your life with Mary)

New series of seminars:

Positiv leben mit den vier Kardinaltugenden
(Live positively with the four cardinal virtues)

Entries:
German Lexicon of authors 2010/2011

Publications:

Kirche heute
(Church nowadays)
Mariological
FATIMA Weltapostolat
Altöttinger Liebfrauenbote

Poem "Christmas" at:
Poem and Society 2010,
Brentano-Gesellschaft , Frankfurt 2009

4 Poems at:
New literature, anthology
August von Goethe Literaturverlag, Frankfurt 2010

Other publications:

„MARIA" –
Ihre Christozentrik im Spiegel der Theologie
(MARIA -
Her Christocentrism in the mirror of theology)
A mariological fundamental book
Published by Verlag Tectum, Marburg 2008

DIE MUSTERFAMILIE
(The Model Family)
A Christian family saga
Published by Books on Demand, Norderstedt 2008

ROSENDUFT DER LIEBE
(Scent of Roses of Love)
A poetry collection with 100 poems
Published by August von Goethe Literaturverlag, Frankfurt 2010

Contact:
www.anna-roth.com

Notizen:

Notizen:

Notizen:

FSC
www.fsc.org
MIX
Papier | Fördert
gute Waldnutzung
FSC® C083411

Zeitfracht Medien GmbH
Ferdinand-Jühlke-Straße 7
99095 Erfurt, Deutschland
produktsicherheit@kolibri360.de